Waiting Is Not Easy!

For Trix.
I can't wait to see what you'll do next.

ISBN 978-1-338-71458-6

12 11 10 9 8 7   22 23 24 25

Printed in the U.S.A.   40

First Scholastic printing, September 2020

This book is set in Century 725/Monotype;
Grilled Cheese BTN/Fontbros

An ELEPHANT & PIGGIE Book

SCHOLASTIC INC.

Waiting Is Not Easy!

By **Mo Willems**

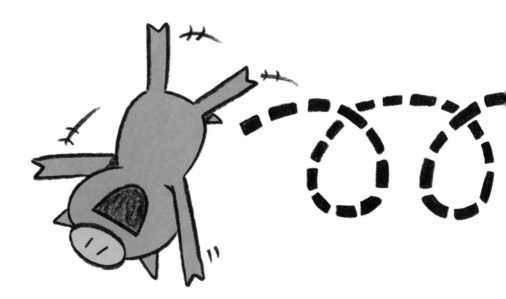

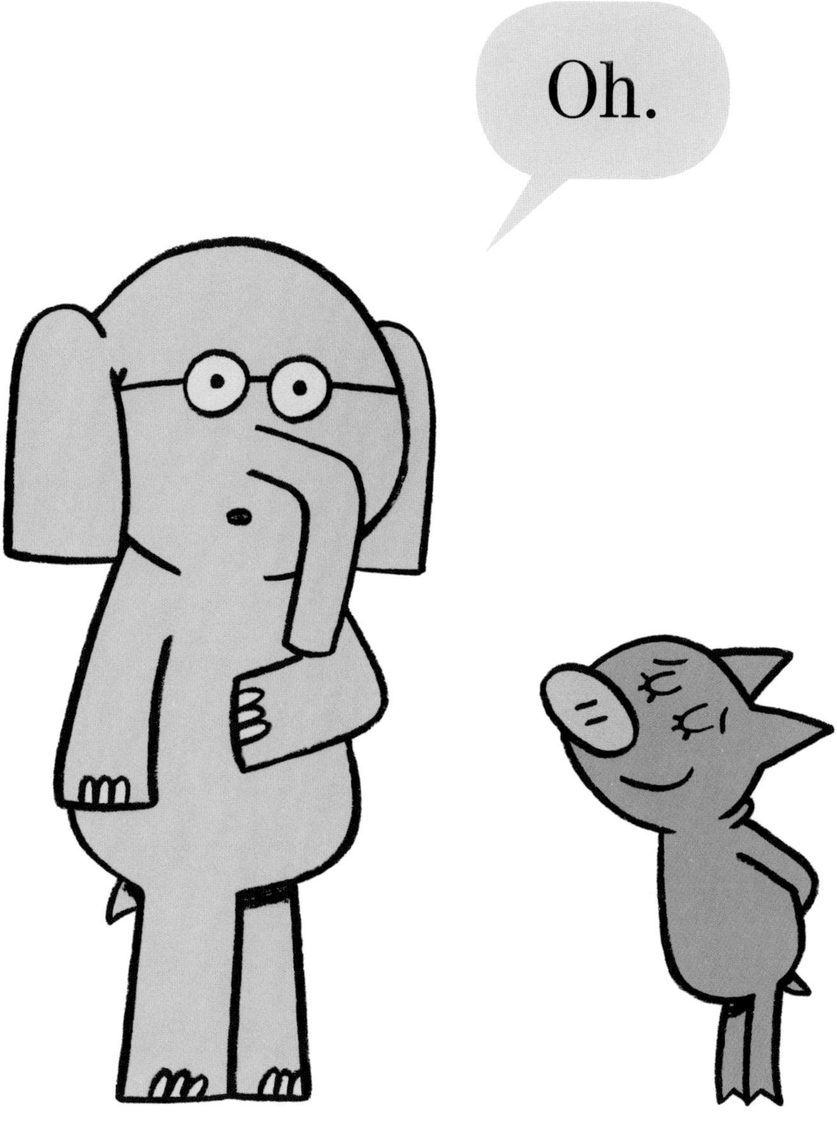
Oh.

9

The surprise
is not
here yet.

Waiting is not easy....

But
we
must
wait.

30

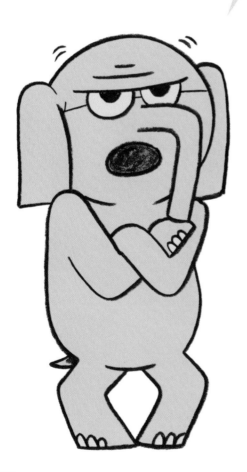

I will not
wait anymore!

Okay. I will wait
some more.

It will be worth it.

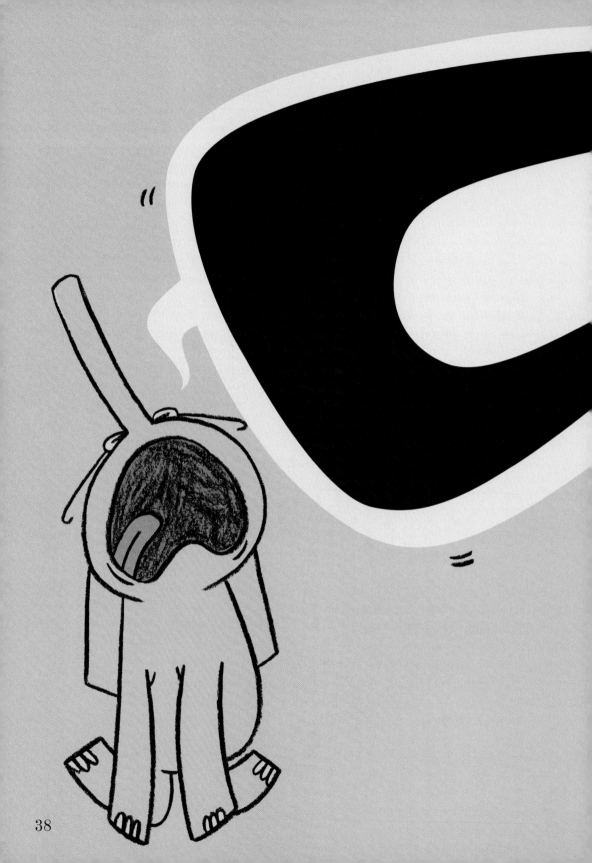

48

waited and waited and waited!

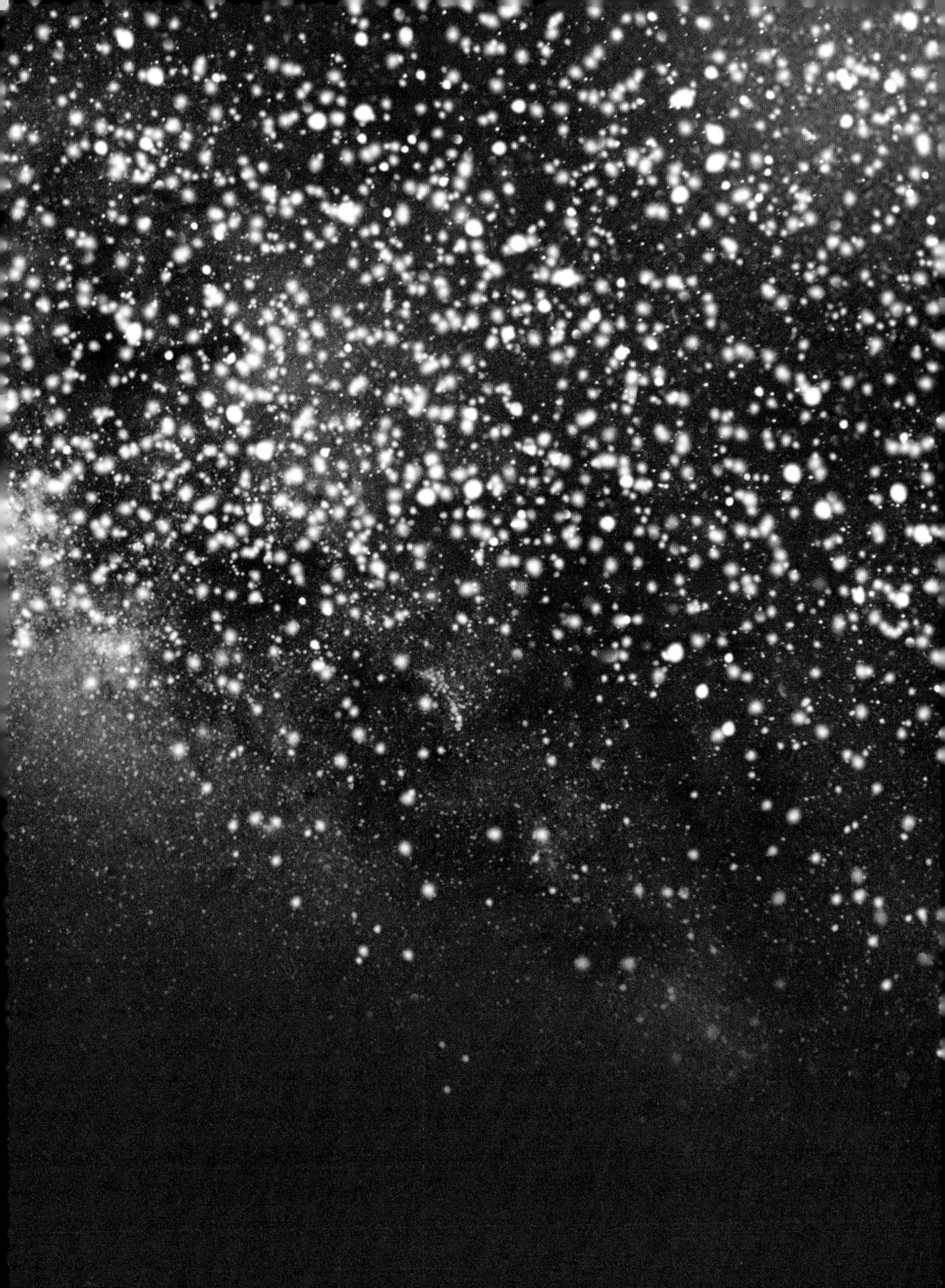

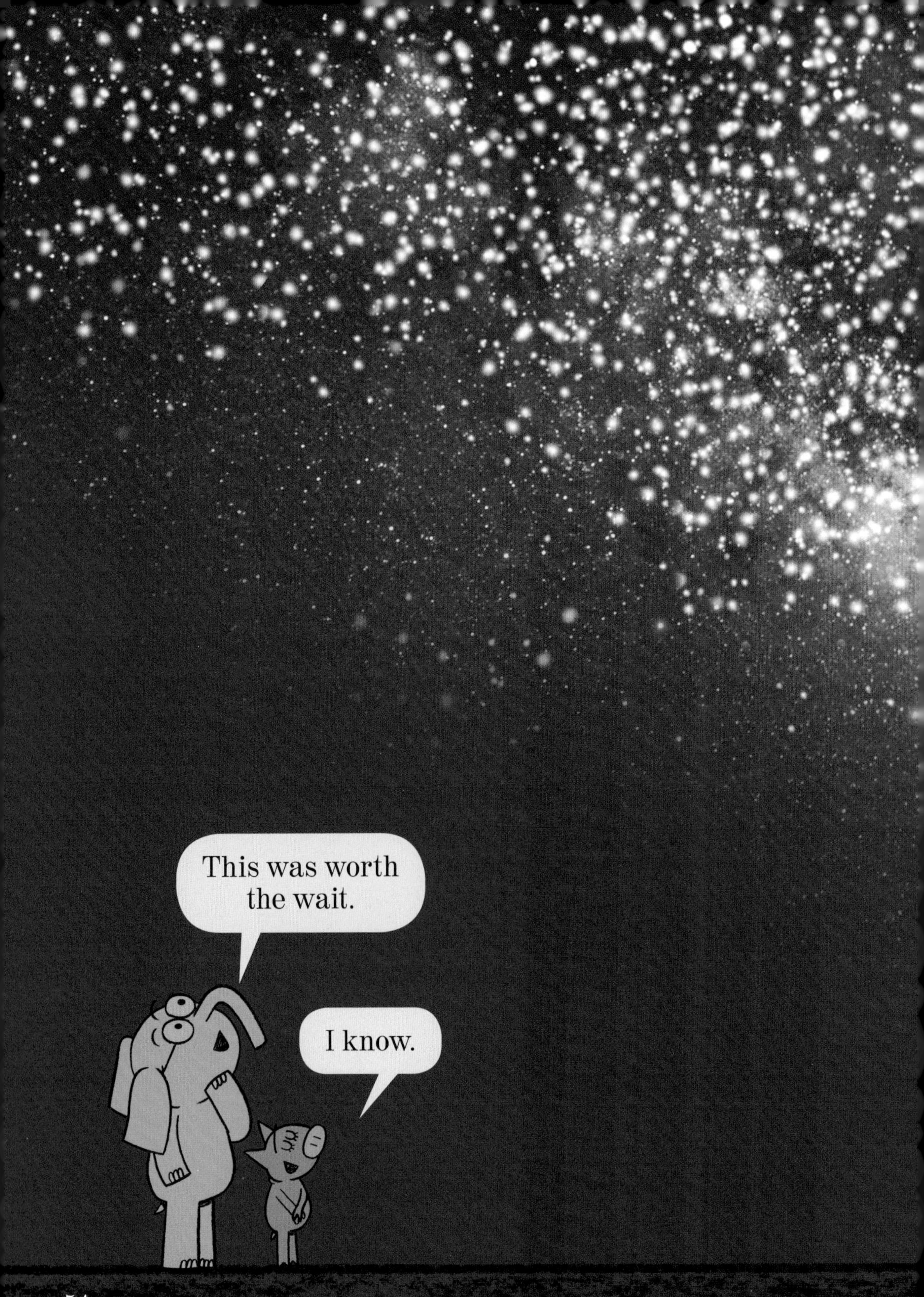
This was worth the wait.
I know.

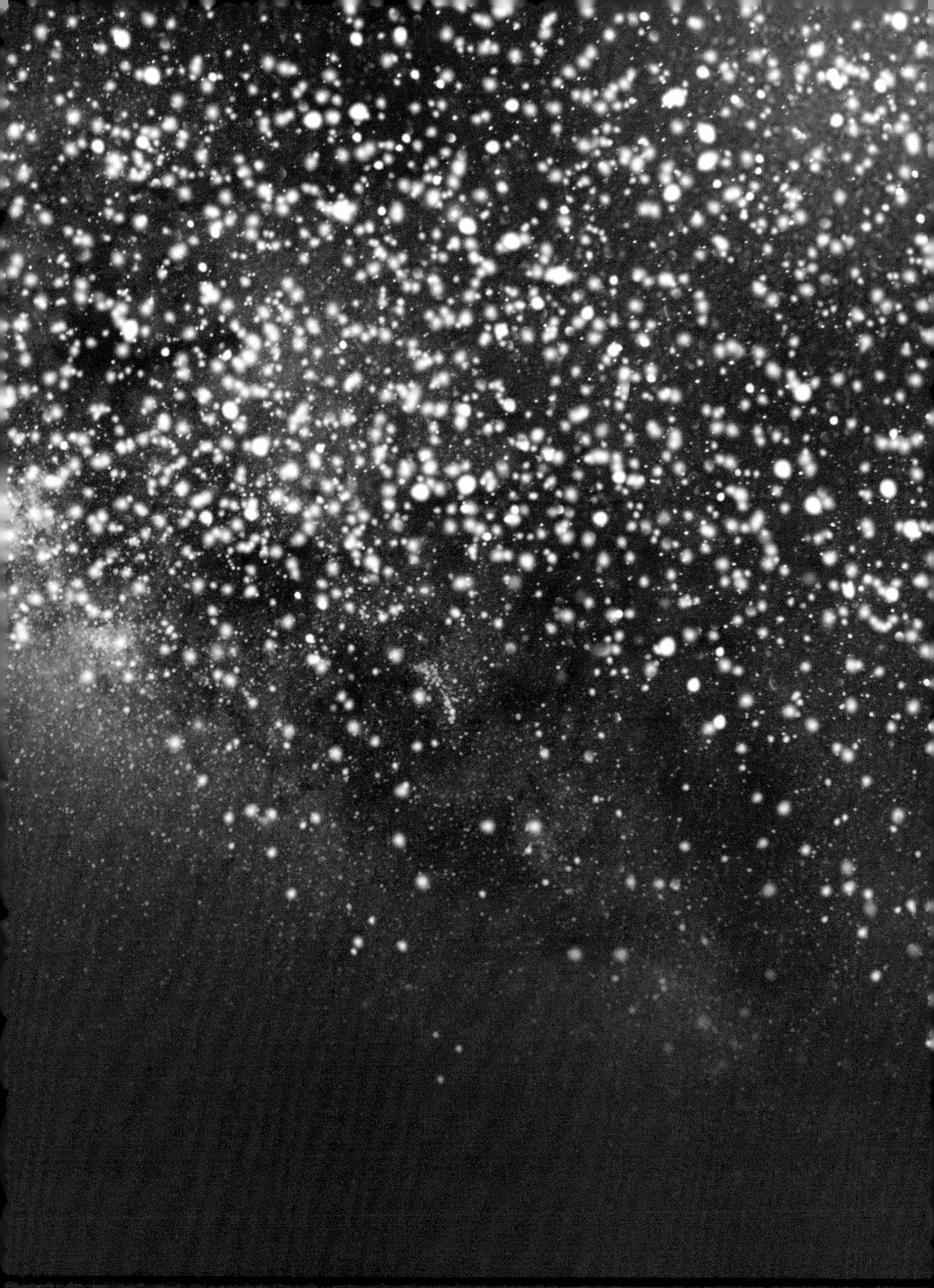

Have you read all of Elephant and Piggie's funny adventures?

Today I Will Fly!

My Friend Is Sad

I Am Invited to a Party!

There Is a Bird on Your Head!
(Theodor Seuss Geisel Medal)

I Love My New Toy!

I Will Surprise My Friend!

Are You Ready to Play Outside?
(Theodor Seuss Geisel Medal)

Watch Me Throw the Ball!

Elephants Cannot Dance!

Pigs Make Me Sneeze!

I Am Going!

Can I Play Too?

We Are in a Book!
(Theodor Seuss Geisel Honor)

I Broke My Trunk!
(Theodor Seuss Geisel Honor)

Should I Share My Ice Cream?

Happy Pig Day!

Listen to My Trumpet!

Let's Go for a Drive!
(Theodor Seuss Geisel Honor)

A Big Guy Took My Ball!
(Theodor Seuss Geisel Honor)

I'm a Frog!

My New Friend Is So Fun!

Waiting Is Not Easy!
(Theodor Seuss Geisel Honor)

I Will Take a Nap!

I *Really* Like Slop!

The Thank You Book